W9-CTJ-818

THE UNTAMED WORLD

Gorillas

Patricia Miller-Schroeder

**RAINTREE
Steck-Vaughn**
PUBLISHERS
The Steck-Vaughn Company

Austin, Texas

M34832658

Published by Raintree Steck-Vaughn Publishers, an imprint of Steck-Vaughn Company.

Library of Congress Cataloging-in-Publication Data
Miller-Schroeder, Patricia.
    Gorillas / Patricia Miller-Schroeder.
        p.   cm. -- (The Untamed world)
    Includes bibliographical references and index.
    Summary: Examines the life of the gorillas, describing their physical features, social behavior, life cycle, and habitat, as well as presenting facts and folklore surrounding these creatures.
    ISBN 0-8172-4562-6
    1. Gorilla--Juvenile literature.   [1. Gorilla.]   I. Title.
II. Series.
QL737.P96M55   1997
599.88'46--dc20

96-21248
CIP
AC

Printed and bound in Canada
1234567890 01 00 99 98 97

Project Editor
Lauri Seidlitz
Design and Illustration
Warren Clark
Project Coordinator
Amanda Woodrow
Raintree Steck-Vaughn Publishers Editor
Kathy DeVico
Copyeditor
Janice Parker
Layout
Chris Bowerman

Consultants
Dr. Pascale Sicotte, formerly with the Karisoke Research Center, now at McMaster University, Ontario, Canada

Dr. Dieter Steklis, Chief Director of International Science with the Dian Fossey Gorilla Fund

Acknowledgments
The publisher wishes to thank Warren Rylands for inspiring this series.

Photograph Credits
Archive Photos: page 46; **Kendra Bond**: pages 5, 37; **Calgary Zoological Society**: pages 12, 29 (Chris Junck); **Corel Corporation**: cover, pages 6, 40, 43, 59, 61; **Brian Keating**: pages 7, 16, 17, 19, 25, 28, 30, 31, 34, 54, 55; **National Zoo**: pages 4, 21, 23 (Jessie Cohen); **Tom Stack and Associates**: pages 10 (Brian Parker), 41 (Joe McDonald), 57 (Warren & Genny Garst); **Visuals Unlimited**: pages 20 (Jane Thomas), 18, 22 (Ken Lucas), 32 (Walt Anderson), 35 (Greg Gorel), 36 (M. Long), 42 (William J. Weber), 44 (A.J. Cunningham); **Helen Winthrop**: pages 8, 24, 26, 27, 60; **John C. Whyte**: page 9.

Contents

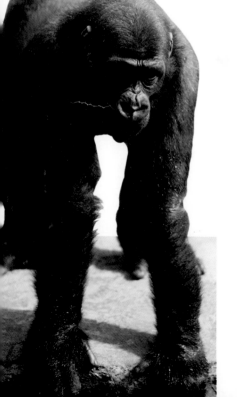

Introduction

When European explorers first visited the jungles of Africa, they brought back stories of a fierce black ape.

People have long been fascinated by gorillas, but they have had many incorrect ideas about how gorillas live. When European explorers first visited the jungles of Africa, they brought back stories of a fierce black ape. Many feared the gorilla's size and strength. Gorillas were often portrayed as monsters in books and movies. Others misunderstood the gorilla's calm nature, believing the gorilla to be slow and dull. Now it is time to learn what gorillas are really like.

In this book, you will read about a gorilla group leader and learn why he is so important. You will learn about the gorilla's famous chest-beating display. You will also discover what scares gorillas the most. Turn the pages, and get ready to discover how these gentle creatures live.

A mixture of strength and gentleness, gorillas have always had the ability to capture our imaginations.

Features

The gorilla is a member of the great ape family, which also includes chimpanzees and orangutans.

Opposite: Gorillas are the largest member of the great ape family.

Have you ever watched a gorilla in a zoo and had it turn to watch you? You may have been surprised at its reaction to you. In fact, you may have wondered exactly who was watching whom! This is not very surprising. **Genetic evidence** shows that humans and gorillas are very similar. Both belong to the same order of animals, the **primates**. The gorilla is a member of the great ape family, which also includes chimpanzees and orangutans. Many people confuse great apes with monkeys, which are also primates. Although apes look a lot like monkeys, none of the great apes have tails, and almost all monkeys have tails.

Although gorillas spend a lot of time resting and eating, this does not mean they are lazy. On the contrary, their size and habits are adaptations to their forest environment.

All gorillas have distinctive facial features.

Size

There is a large size difference between male and female gorillas. Wild male gorillas can weigh 300 to 400 pounds (135 to 180 kg). Adult females usually weigh about half as much as adult males. They range from 150 to 250 pounds (68 to 113 kg). Adult males can be 5.5 to 6 feet (1.7 to 1.8 m) tall, with an arm span that stretches from 7.5 to 8.5 feet (2.3 to 2.6 m). Female gorillas are shorter, with a smaller arm span. Gorillas living in zoos are often heavier than those in the wild because they get less exercise. Some zoo gorillas weigh more than 600 pounds (270 kg)!

Males and females are similar in size and weight until they are about eight years old. At that time, males put on a great deal of weight. By the time males are 12 years old, they weigh twice as much as females.

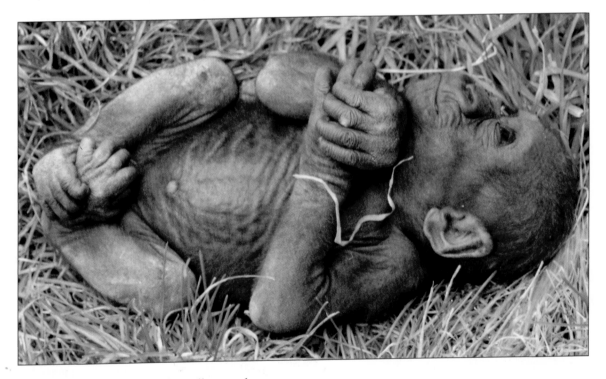

Despite the large size of adult gorillas, newborn gorillas weigh only 3 to 4 pounds (1.4 to 1.8 kg), which is half the weight of most human babies.

Skin and Hair

When gorillas are born, their skin is a pink, pinkish-gray, or light brown color. Some have pink spots on the soles of their feet and hands. As they grow, their skin turns black on areas where there is little hair, such as their face, ears, fingers, and chest.

Silver-colored fur on the back of a gorilla is a sign that it is a mature male that most likely has his own group.

The hair of gorillas is mostly black. On some gorillas, it is a rich blue-black color. Others may have some gray, brown, or red overtones in their hair. When a male gorilla is 11 or 12 years old, the hair on a saddle-shaped area on his back turns a silver color. This silver saddle means the male has reached sexual maturity. This shows other gorillas that the male is old enough to lead a group and to mate. When male gorillas reach this age, they are called **silverbacks**. When gorillas get old, the hair on their head and shoulders sometimes turns gray.

The species of gorillas living in mountain areas usually has longer and thicker hair than those living in the warmer lowlands. Some gorillas look quite bushy and have long hair on their heads. Other gorillas may have hair so short that they seem to have a crew cut!

LIFE SPAN

Wild gorillas may live for 35 to 45 years. However, the chance of them dying before they live this long is quite high. Like other wild animals, many gorillas die young. Some scientists estimate that 35 to 40 percent of young gorillas die as infants or juveniles. Some gorilla deaths are the result of accidents or disease. Many wild gorillas are killed by poachers or hunters. In captivity, gorillas generally live longer because they do not face as many dangers, and can receive medical attention. One captive gorilla lived to be well over 50 years old.

Special Adaptations

Gorillas have many special features that help them survive in their natural environment in the forests of Africa.

Gorillas rely on their senses of sight and touch to help them find food.

Hands

A gorilla's hands are much like our own. They have four flexible fingers and an **opposable** thumb. They can use their fingers and thumb to pick up or hang onto objects, to pull off leaves and other plant parts while feeding, and to pick small objects out of their hair when grooming. Gorillas also use their hands to hang onto branches when climbing, and to build nests.

Like humans, gorillas have tiny raised ridges, or fingerprints, on the tips of their fingers. These ridges help gorillas feel and hang onto objects.

Smell

Gorillas rely on their sense of smell to warn them of something unusual in their environment. If they do not recognize an odor, or if it makes them uneasy, they will use their eyes to find what is making the smell.

Hearing

Gorillas have a well-developed sense of hearing. If they hear a sound they do not recognize, or one that alarms them, they will look to see where the sound is coming from. Many people studying gorillas have noted that the human voice is the one sound that almost always causes gorillas to run away.

Teeth and Skull

The gorilla's teeth and skull are adapted to eating tough plants. Their skulls are large and heavy. Male gorillas and some large females have bony ridges on top of their heads called **sagittal crests**. The big muscles that move their lower jaw are attached to the sagittal crest. Gorilla jaws are made of thick, sturdy bone. Their molar teeth are broad and flat. Their teeth are strong enough to crush and chew tough plants, like nettles and wild celery. Males have large canine teeth that may be used for display or fighting.

Sight

Gorillas have good eyesight. They notice even slight movements around them. Their eyes are located in the front of their head. This allows them to judge distance and depth when moving through the trees and vines of the forest. Gorillas can see in color.

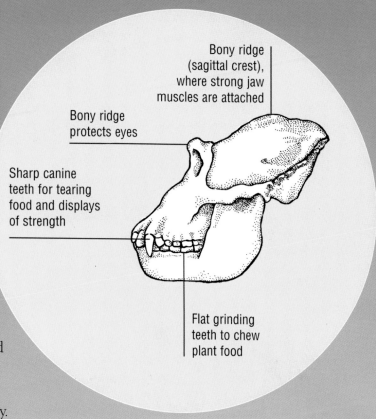

Bony ridge (sagittal crest), where strong jaw muscles are attached

Bony ridge protects eyes

Sharp canine teeth for tearing food and displays of strength

Flat grinding teeth to chew plant food

Gorilla Faces

Gorillas have low foreheads, with bony ridges that stick out over their eyes. Their face shapes can be round, oval, or long. They can be flat, or have a jaw that sticks out.

Gorilla noses are distinctive. Each of the three subspecies of gorillas has a different nose shape. Even within a small group of the same subspecies, noses can look quite different.

Feet

A gorilla's big toes are opposable, meaning that like thumbs, they can move toward or away from the other toes. This gives the gorilla the ability to use its feet for grasping. Adult gorillas sometimes use their feet to steady themselves on a branch when climbing. Infants are even better at using their feet to grasp objects. They use their feet to hang onto their mother's hair.

When walking, gorillas can either stick out their toes or curl them under the soles of their feet. This makes a big difference in the size of their footprints.

Movement

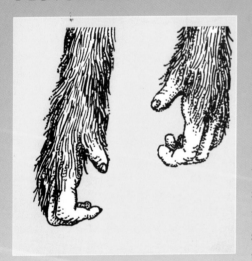

On the ground, gorillas usually move on all four limbs. They use a special kind of movement called **knuckle-walking**. To knuckle-walk, the gorilla's feet are flat on the ground, while its weight is carried on the backs of its fingers. The powerful arms of gorillas are longer than their legs. This keeps them almost upright when they knuckle-walk. Gorillas can move for short distances on two legs. This might happen if they are putting on a display of their size or strength, or carrying something that needs two hands.

Gorillas spend most of their time on the ground. However, they sometimes climb trees to rest or feed. Smaller females and juveniles climb trees more often than the large males. Gorillas move cautiously in the trees. When danger approaches, they drop to the ground and run away. Gorillas usually move slowly and take many feeding breaks. When moving from one area to another, they travel at speeds of 2 to 5 miles per hour (3 to 8 kph). If they have to run, they can reach speeds of 15 to 20 miles per hour (25 to 33 kph) over short distances.

Classification

Gorillas belong to a large order of animals called primates. This order includes monkeys, apes, humans, and prosimians, a group of distant relatives that includes lemurs. Gorillas are the largest living primate. Most monkeys are smaller than apes. The smallest primates are the tiny mouse lemurs. These prosimian primates weigh only about 2 ounces (60 g). Compare this to a large gorilla's 400 pounds (180 kg)!

THE PRIMATES

Anthropoids

Marmosets & Tamarins	Great Apes	Lesser Apes	Old World Monkeys	New World Monkeys

Tamarin	*Chimpanzee*	*Gibbon*	*Baboon*	*Spider Monkey*
• 17 species • Small animals like squirrels • Live in South and Central American forests	• 4 species • Include chimpanzees, gorillas, orangutans • Are largest primates	• 6 species • Live in Southeast Asia • Long, slender arms to help them swing from branch to branch • Include gibbons and siamangs	• 80 species • Live in Africa and Asia • Most have tails; some do not • Include colobus monkeys, macaques, mangabeys, baboons, langurs, patas monkeys	• 30 species • Live in South and Central America • Include capuchin monkeys, squirrel monkeys, spider monkeys

Prosimians

Ring-tailed Lemur

Lemurs	Bush babies	Lorises	Tarsiers
• 17 species • All live in Madagascar	• 6 species • Live in African forests	• 5 species • Live in Southeast Asia and Africa	• 3 species • Live on islands in Southeast Asia

Mountain and Lowland Gorillas

There is only one species of gorilla (*Gorilla gorilla*) living today in Africa. Scientists divide gorillas into three subspecies. All three subspecies live in the rain forest, and all look similar, although each subspecies has slightly different characteristics.

Western Lowland Gorilla (*Gorilla gorilla gorilla*)

- Most widespread species
- Lives in the lowland rain forests of Nigeria, Cameroon, Rio Muni, Gabon, the Central African Republic, and the Republic of Congo
- Shortest in height and lightest in weight
- Often has gray or reddish hair on its head and shoulders
- Broad face and skull
- Short hair
- Most common zoo gorilla

Eastern Lowland Gorilla (*Gorilla gorilla graueri*)

- Small population
- Live only in Zaire
- Tallest and heaviest of the gorillas
- Mainly black, some grayish-colored hair
- Long, narrow face and skull
- Short hair
- Rarely seen in zoos

Mountain Gorilla (*Gorilla gorilla beringei*)

- Small populations in the cold, damp highlands of the Virunga Volcanoes, on the borders of Zaire, Rwanda, and Uganda; also found in Uganda's Bwindi-Impenetrable Forest.
- Large and heavy, but smaller than Eastern Lowland Gorillas
- Hair is thick, glossy black, and long
- Most studied of all gorillas
- None currently living in zoos

The Group

In the group, young gorillas learn how to survive and get along with other gorillas.

Opposite: A healthy gorilla group will have at least two adult females with their infants and juveniles, as well as the silverback. Bonds among the gorillas in a group are very strong.

The group provides gorillas with protection, companions, and playmates.

Gorillas live in social groups that are in many ways like families. The group is very important to them. Any gorillas without a group will do their best to either join one or start a new one.

Living together is safer for gorillas. Group members can spot predators and give alarm calls. Mother gorillas caring for their youngsters get help from other females. Many male gorillas help protect and care for young ones.

During the day the group travels and feeds together. At night they sleep close together in their nests. In the group, young gorillas learn how to survive and get along with other gorillas. Even zoo gorillas are happier when they live in groups.

Group Composition

Gorilla groups usually have 5 to 20 members, although larger groups are sometimes seen. The leader of each group is a large silverback male. There will be at least two adult females in a group. The silverback leader will mate with most or all of the adult females in his group. Most female gorillas change groups as they become adults. Sometimes they will change groups many times, looking for the best group in which to raise their young.

The silverback male is the father of most of the young gorillas in his group.

Young males usually leave the group when they become adults. They wander alone, or with other males until they can form their own group. Sometimes they will challenge the silverback of a group to see if he is able to defend his females. If the younger male is lucky, he may be able to lure a few females away.

In addition to the silverback and females, a gorilla group will have juveniles and infants. There may also be some young **blackback** or silverback males. These younger males may be related to the leader. They may sometimes mate with the females if the silverback is not around.

Life in the Group

Life in a gorilla group is peaceful and friendly. Group members will nap with or groom one another during rest periods. Females will serve as "aunts" for one another's youngsters. Play groups form around the silverback, who is often the center of attention. There is rarely any fighting within the group. The silverback can stop most squabbles by simply standing still and glaring at the troublemakers. This is a message to the other gorillas that they should behave themselves.

Gorillas are usually even-tempered and quiet. However, within each group, there will be some gorillas who are more nervous, calm, shy, or aggressive than others. The personality of the silverback affects the lives of all of the other gorillas in the group.

The silverback is the group's decision-maker. Each day, he decides where the group will go to feed. He also decides when to travel to other areas, and when the group will stop for the night. The silverback is also the group's main defender. When danger threatens, he will place himself between the danger and his family.

Young gorillas help form bonds among group members. All members of the group care for and protect the young.

Seasonal Activities

Life in the rain forest does not change much from season to season. There is plenty of lush, green vegetation to eat all year-round. The types of plants available to eat can change depending on the season. Gorilla groups travel around their **home range**, or territory, to wherever the best food is growing at the time.

Gorillas are most active early in the day and late in the afternoon. When the group wakes in the morning, they will feed and travel for about 3 hours. In the middle of the day, they will stop and rest for 2 or 3 hours. Young gorillas often play during the rest period. After resting, the group will travel and feed until late afternoon. At dusk, the entire group will build nests and settle down for the night.

Nests

All gorillas learn to build nests early in their life. Nests are made by bending branches and plants into a rough circular shape. They are made on the ground or in low trees, depending on the size of the gorilla. Nest sizes vary from about 2 to 5 feet (.6 to 1.5 m) in diameter.

Day nests can be as simple as a few plants and branches placed on the ground.

Most gorillas make two nests each day—one nest for their daytime rest, and one for their nighttime sleep. The day nest is not as sturdy as the night nest. Each gorilla makes its own nest, although young gorillas sleep with their mothers until they are about three years old. Young gorillas will practice making nests as early as eight months of age. Sometimes they will sleep in a nest they have made close to their mother. Male gorillas occasionally share their nests with young orphaned gorillas. Their body heat helps to keep the young orphans warm.

Fun and Games

Play is very important to young gorillas. It allows them to test their strength and learn about being a gorilla. The rain forest provides a real adventure playground. Young gorillas are excellent tree climbers. They love to swing from low branches and vines.

Young gorillas usually play in the center of the group. Here they are surrounded by adults that will protect them. Adults are very good-natured about the youngsters' play. They will let young gorillas climb and jump on them. One game is sliding down an adult gorilla's body. Other games that gorillas enjoy are wrestling, tumbling, chasing, and play-fighting. Gorilla observers have called a favorite game "King of the Hill." In this game, young gorillas try to knock one another off a hill or stump. The one who can stay on the hill is the winner, or "king."

Games of young gorillas often involve imitating or practicing adult skills. They may break small branches and practice nest-building. In this way, the young gorillas are learning skills they will need when they get older.

Young gorillas spend most of their time exploring and playing. Even adult gorillas play occasionally.

Communication

Gorillas are very intelligent animals that have many different ways of communicating. They use different **vocalizations**, body language, and displays to send messages to one another.

Vocalizations

Like people, gorillas sneeze, cough, yawn, hiccup, burp, and laugh. They also have at least 17 different vocalizations. Some are used more often than others. The most common is a belch that sounds like someone clearing his or her throat. When one animal gives a rumbling belch, it will be answered by others to show that they feel content.

A sharp pig-grunt noise is a common sound that means the gorilla is annoyed. It might be heard when a mother scolds an infant, or a silverback stops a squabble. A hoot-bark sound shows curiosity or mild alarm. It is often used by the silverback to alert the group. A series of grunts may be used to keep group members together. Barks and screams are heard when gorillas fight. The male leaders from different groups give a special "Hoo-Hoo-Hoo" series of calls when they are close to one another. These calls can be heard for up to a half mile (.8 km) away. They are answered by the males of other groups. In this way, the groups can avoid one another.

When gorillas see humans, they make sounds like roars and screams to warn the group. When gorillas are very frightened, and when danger is very close, they suddenly become very quiet. The sudden silence tells the rest of the group that danger is near, without giving away the location of the group.

A gorilla will often come face-to-face with another gorilla in order to get its attention.

Body Language

Gorillas also use body language to communicate. To show excitement, they may slap their chests or the ground. They may also tear up plants or break branches. When gorillas shake their heads, it means they are going to put on a display.

To show anger or aggression, a gorilla may stare, turn its head sharply, lunge, or bluff charge. In a bluff charge, one gorilla runs toward another, but stops a few feet away. If this does not work, the gorilla may wrestle with or bite the other gorilla. It is rare for aggressive behavior to go past a stare or a lunge.

Gorillas also have many ways of showing that they mean no harm. A gorilla may turn its head and face away from a threatening animal. It can crouch down, lower its head, and tuck its arms and legs under its body. This submissive behavior will usually stop aggression from other gorillas.

Displays

Gorillas have a very impressive chest-beating display that means they are very excited. It is usually done by adult males. The display starts with a series of hoots. The gorilla then rises on its hind legs, throws plants in the air, and kicks upward with one leg. Next, it beats its chest with its hands, making a loud "Pok-Pok-Pok" sound. The gorilla then runs sideways, tearing up plants and slapping the ground.

Even infants only four months old will pound their chests. However, only adult males will make hoot calls. The display is sometimes done to scare others. It is also done to get attention or to relieve stress.

Adult male gorillas beat their chests to make a threat, or to release some energy. When younger gorillas practice beating their chests, it often just means that they want to play.

Gorilla Young

Young gorillas help form social bonds among group members.

Opposite: By the time young gorillas are two years old, they are confident enough to follow their group on their own.

Shortly after a gorilla infant is born, the mother cleans it and puts it on her chest. The infant will then nuzzle around and begin to nurse.

When morning comes, the other group members will be very interested in the new group member. Watching an infant is one way other female gorillas learn how to be mothers. At first, the mother is very protective of her infant. Before too long, however, she will let the others look at and gently touch her infant. Young gorillas are very important members of the group because they help form social bonds among group members.

Gorillas usually have only one infant at a time. From birth, the infants are alert and curious.

Birth

The **gestation** time for gorillas is 8.5 months. Shortly before giving birth, the mother becomes restless and builds a nest. Most wild gorilla births take place at night. Night is a good time for a gorilla to give birth because the whole group will be resting together for several hours.

Gorillas give birth to only one infant at a time. Births may be during any month of the year. The mother will care for her infant for many years. She will not give birth again until the youngster is four or five years old.

Infants

Gorilla infants are small and helpless at birth. Their wrinkled faces are pinkish-colored. Their ears are large and stick out from their heads. The infants' brown eyes are open and curious shortly after birth. They have long, skinny arms and legs. Despite their small size, however, gorilla infants are quite strong. Their hands and feet can grasp their mother's hair shortly after birth. In fact, they can support their weight hanging from one hand for over 3 minutes.

As tiny as they are, infant gorillas are quite sturdy. Before learning how to ride on its mother's back, an infant gorilla will be carried along while the mother feeds.

For the first 3 months, the youngster clings to its mother's chest and upper abdomen while she sits or travels. When it is older, the youngster will ride on her back.

Care

The mother gorilla carries her infant wherever she goes for several months. She must keep the infant warm until it grows its longer coat. Newborn gorillas are dependent on their mothers' milk for nourishment. It is the only food they will eat for the first 6 to 8 months. They will gradually begin to try different bits of plant food. They learn about different foods by tasting what their mother is eating. Young gorillas will continue to nurse long after they are eating plant food. Some may drink milk for 3 to 4 years, if their mothers will allow it.

During the early months of a gorilla's life, its mother will be its most important protector and teacher. As it gets older, other group members also become very important. When a young gorilla is 8 to 12 months old, it will join play groups of other young gorillas.

The large silverback male, usually the father of all the young gorillas in the group, is often tolerant of youngsters. They will play around him, or even on him. The silverback is also very protective of the young gorillas, and keeps a watchful eye on them as they tumble about.

Development

1 – 4 Months

Infant

Gorillas weigh 3 to 4 pounds (1.4 to 1.8 kg) at birth. They have sparse black hair on their bodies, and they have a white tuft of hair on their rumps. From its pinkish color at birth, a gorilla infant's skin turns to black within 2 months. The infant clings to its mother's abdomen, and she supports it with one hand while she moves. Infants rely on their mother's milk for their food.

The first few years in a gorilla's life are a time to learn many important things, such as what to eat, how to build nests, how to climb trees, and how to avoid danger.

4 Months – 1 Year

Infant

By 12 months of age, infants weigh 15 to 20 pounds (6.8 to 9 kg). Hair grows thicker on their bodies, and black hair grows on their heads. At 12 months, infants will regularly ride on their mothers' backs and will eat plants. Infants often try chest-beating when they are as young as four months old.

1 Year – 3 Years

Infant

Infants are **weaned** by two years of age. They weigh about 60 pounds (27 kg) by three and a half years of age. During this time, they become more independent. They will often join in play groups away from their mother.

3 Years – 8 Years

Juvenile

Juveniles weigh about 120 pounds (54 kg) by five years of age. The white tuft of hair on their rumps disappears by the time they are four years old. They build and sleep in their own nests. They wrestle, climb, and play rowdy games.

8 – 12 Years

Blackback Male

At this stage, males are called blackbacks. They weigh the same as females until they are eight years old, when they grow much larger.

12+ Years

Silverback Male

Males grow a silver saddle-shaped patch on their backs, beginning at 11 or 12 years of age. They are able to breed at this age and will be fully mature at 15 years.

8+ Years

Adult Female

Adult females weigh 150 to 250 pounds (68 to 113 kg). They are ready to mate when they are 7 or 8 years old.

Silverback gorillas are easy to recognize because of their large size as well as the silver-colored fur on their backs.

Habitat

Mountain gorillas can be found in forests 11,000 feet (3,353 m) or more above sea level.

Gorillas are found only in the lush, wet forests of West and Central Africa. This area provides many different plants for gorillas to eat all year. Some gorillas live in tropical, lowland rain forests, where the temperature can go up to 90°F (32°C). Others live in the evergreen mountain forests, or dense bamboo forests. Mountain gorillas can be found in forests 11,000 feet (3,353 m) or more above sea level. Temperatures in these mountains can drop to below freezing at night.

Opposite: Forest habitats provide gorillas with plenty of food and nesting sites.

Mountain gorillas in Rwanda can be difficult to see in their lush, forested environment.

Home Range

Gorilla groups have home ranges about 5 square miles (13 sq km) in size. The groups eat and travel throughout their home range. The boundaries of home ranges are flexible. Home ranges of different gorilla groups sometimes overlap. If this happens, the gorillas do not have to fight over food. There are plenty of plants to eat in the rain forest.

Gorillas traveling through their home ranges often use the same trails many times. You can tell where gorillas have traveled because they trample a wide path through the dense vegetation. Bent leaves and branches show the direction the group has traveled. There may be knuckleprints and footprints in the dirt along the path. These trails often lead to favorite feeding and nesting sites.

Gorillas often travel single file along the trails they have made between favorite feeding sites. Lowland gorillas usually travel longer distances than mountain gorillas to find their best feeding sites. At higher altitudes, mountain gorillas find more food within reach.

Viewpoints

In an overcrowded country, should land be set aside to protect endangered gorillas?

The small country of Rwanda has a population of 7 million people. Volcanoes National Park in Rwanda is a 48 square mile (125 sq km) forest sanctuary for about 200 mountain gorillas. The park is surrounded by many people. The Rwandan government has created a program to both help the gorillas and raise money for their poor country. Tourists pay large sums of money to see the mountain gorillas in their natural habitat. However, the recent civil war in Rwanda has disrupted the tourist program. Many people have been left without homes, and they are desperate for living space.

PRO  **CON**

1 The mountain gorilla conservation project has brought a great deal of money into the country. Tourism is the country's third largest cash source. Local people get jobs such as guides, wardens, and educators. Local businesses benefit from the tourist money.

2 The people of Rwanda are proud of their role in conserving the rare mountain gorilla. Many people have risked their lives to help protect the gorillas.

1 People are starving because there is not enough land for them to raise their own food or herd animals. More people would benefit from growing crops or raising cattle than would benefit from gorilla tourism.

2 When the park was formed, land had to be taken away from some people. These people are no longer allowed to use the land to hunt or herd their animals. The needs of people should come before the needs of gorillas.

Food

Scientists have discovered that gorillas eat over 100 different types of plants.

Gorillas use their hands and teeth to carefully eat different parts of various plants. They will eat the bark or roots of some plants, and the stems, leaves, or berries of others.

Gorillas are **herbivores**, which means they eat only plants. Their habitat provides them with a wide variety of plants to eat. Scientists have discovered that gorillas eat over 100 different types of plants. Some favorite foods are wild celery, thistles, nettles, bamboo shoots, blackberries, and ferns. However, the largest part of a gorilla's diet is leaves, shoots, and stems. Gorillas can therefore also be called **folivores**, which are animals that eat mainly leaves.

Lowland gorillas eat more fruit than mountain gorillas. This is because more fruit is found in the forests where lowland gorillas live. However, fruits are only available at certain times and places. This means lowland gorillas may travel farther than mountain gorillas when feeding.

Many of the plants that gorillas like to eat taste bitter to humans. Some of the plants, such as nettles and thistles, have barbs or stinging parts. These do not seem to bother the gorillas. Gorillas often prepare their food by wiping off stings or peeling back outer layers.

Other Foods

Gorillas do not usually eat meat. Even if they find a dead animal or bird sitting on a nest, they leave it alone. They will sometimes eat insects, snails, and slugs. Gorillas have been observed digging up ant nests and eating the ants inside. When they do this, they must put up with the ants' stings. There have also been reports of gorillas eating honey from wild beehives. Plants, however, are the gorilla's main food.

Wild gorillas do not seem to drink water. There are not many permanent streams where gorillas live. However, their habitat is very moist. They may get enough water from the dew and rain on the plants they eat. The plants themselves are often juicy and contain moisture. This seems to provide gorillas with all the water they need.

Like many other plant-eaters, gorillas spend much of their time looking for food and eating.

When gorillas eat, they usually sit down, with their bellies sticking out between their legs. Gorillas then eat what they like from the food in arm's reach. When they are tired of one area, they move on to the next site. Each gorilla finds its own food. Only young gorillas sometimes get help. Although their large bellies make them look fat, gorillas are actually very strong and muscular.

Potbellied Apes

Gorillas often look fat or potbellied. This is because of the large amount of bulky vegetation they eat. The types of plants a gorilla eats have a lot of fiber. This food is stored in the gorilla's huge stomach while it is digesting. Gorillas must eat huge amounts of food each day to get enough nutrients. Fortunately, gorillas are surrounded by food. They do not have to move a lot to get enough to fill their stomachs.

When bamboo shoots are in season, silverbacks can eat as much as 75 pounds (34 kg) each day. The smaller females will eat about 40 pounds (18 kg). After eating for several hours, gorillas will rest to let their food digest.

Mountain Gorillas in the Food Cycle

A food cycle shows how energy in the form of food is passed from one living thing to another. Gorillas survive by eating plants. As they feed, and as they move through the forest, gorillas affect the lives of many other animals.

As they move through the jungle, gorillas help clear a path for animals such as the African buffalo.

Very rarely, a predator such as a leopard will catch and eat a young or very old gorilla.

Gorillas break branches and twigs, drop fruit, and peel strips of vegetation when they feed. This supplies food for smaller creatures, such as ants.

Gorillas provide a home for parasites such as the hookworm.

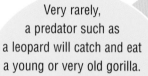

Sometimes gorillas will eat ants, ant eggs, or slugs and grubs.

Undigested seeds in gorilla droppings help spread seeds from one part of their habitat to another. This ensures a continuing food supply for themselves and others.

Gorillas eat mainly plants, such as wild celery, thistle, bark, bamboo, and fungus.

Wildlife Biologists Talk About Gorillas

Dian Fossey

"The next two decades are estimated to see the extinction of twenty species of animals. Human beings must decide now whether or not the mountain gorilla will become one of them, a species discovered and extinct within the same century."

Dian Fossey studied mountain gorillas in Rwanda from 1966 until 1985. She set up the Karisoke Research Center to study gorillas, and she uncovered many new facts about gorilla society. Dr. Fossey published several articles and a book, *Gorillas in the Mist*, about her work with gorillas.

George Schaller

"No one who looks into a gorilla's eyes—intelligent, gentle, vulnerable—can remain unchanged, for the gap between ape and human vanishes."

George Schaller conducted the first in-depth field study of mountain gorillas in 1959. His observations about gorillas have been published in scientific journals and in books, including *The Mountain Gorilla* and *The Year of the Gorilla*. He has studied and written books on many other endangered species, including African lions, Bengal tigers, and giant pandas.

Dieter Steklis

"Virtually everyone who has worked with gorillas feels an indescribable sense of awe, mixed with fear, and yet feels trust and unmistakable community when in their presence."

Dieter Steklis was director of the Karisoke Research Center in Rwanda from 1991 to 1993, where he studied mountain gorilla communication. He has edited or written 53 publications on primates.

Competition

Opposite: Although the gorilla is capable of impressive displays, it is normally very calm, and generally tolerant of other animals in its surroundings.

Gorillas are usually easygoing animals. For centuries, they lived in an environment where food and living space were plentiful. There was no need to compete with other gorillas or even with other animals for food. These giant apes are so large that they do not have to worry about predators. There are very few predators that would risk the anger of adult gorillas by attacking the group. The gorilla has only one serious competitor—human beings. Humans compete with gorillas for habitat, and kill gorillas for food and profit.

Gorillas will show their canine teeth and make loud noises when they are angry or when they want to scare off an intruder.

Challenges from Other Gorillas

Gorillas do not need to compete with one another for food. There is usually more than enough for all. However, there is competition among male gorillas for females. Males within the same group may compete for females, but more often the challenge comes from males outside the group. These males may try to get females to leave their old group and join them. An outsider silverback male may even kill an infant in an attempt to mate with its mother. The group silverback plays a very important role in protecting his young from these and other dangers.

The silverback male can be playful and tolerant with younger gorillas.
He is respected by the rest of the group and will use his size and
dominant behavior to keep all group members in line.

Relationships with Other Animals

Gorillas share their habitat with many other animals. Depending on where they live in Africa, these animals can include: elephants, small antelope, buffalo, monkeys, and chimpanzees. In almost all cases, gorillas do not pay any attention to the other animals. They go about their business and let the other animals go about theirs.

Some of the animals eat the same plants as gorillas. There are a lot of these plants, so this is not usually a problem. Even when two animals eat the same plants, they do not always eat the same parts. For example, gorillas and buffalo both like to eat nettles. Buffalo nip off the tender tops, while gorillas like the roots, stems, and leaves.

Some animals use the trails made by gorillas to help them get around in the forest. Buffalo will follow gorilla groups closely as they travel through the dense plants. Gorillas sometimes bluff charge the buffalo. It has been observed that gorillas seem to enjoy scattering the buffalo in all directions.

Chimpanzees are the only apes that will hunt and regularly eat meat. Even when they share a gorilla's habitat, they do not compete for food.

43

Competing with Humans

Although gorillas live peacefully with most other animals, they are often in competition with humans. Large numbers of people live in the parts of Africa where gorillas live. People sometimes see the forests where the gorillas live as wasted land that could be used better for farming. Some people destroy the forest by running their cattle through it.

In countries where wood is the only fuel that is available for warmth and cooking, the forest trees are in great demand. In some areas, the gorillas themselves are regularly hunted and eaten. Gorillas are even killed in national reserves where they are supposed to be protected by laws.

Many rain forests around the world have been burned or cut down to increase agricultural space for humans. In addition to the loss of plant and animal species, the loss of rain forests may also cause global climatic changes.

Decline in Population

Gorilla populations are declining for several reasons. Two of the worst problems facing gorillas are habitat loss and **poaching**.

The gorilla's forest home has always provided for all of its needs. Pressure from humans, however, is now causing gorilla habitat to shrink. People want to cut the forest down to make room for farms and mines, or to get lumber. Gorillas will not go very far into open woodlands or grasslands. They cannot swim, so streams and rivers form another habitat boundary. When rain forests are destroyed, gorillas are trapped in small pockets of forest. They can no longer wander freely around their home range. As farms appear closer to their homes, gorillas may raid crops and come into conflict with people.

All gorilla populations are declining because of poaching. In the western lowlands of Africa, large numbers of gorillas are being killed for food. Much of this food feeds the work crews who are cutting down the forests.

Conservation efforts in poor countries work only if local people will benefit from the conservation. Rwanda has created a tourism industry around the gorilla. Many foreigners will pay a lot of money to see the gorilla in its natural habitat. Rwanda's currency now features a picture of the gorilla, showing the animal's importance to the country's economy.

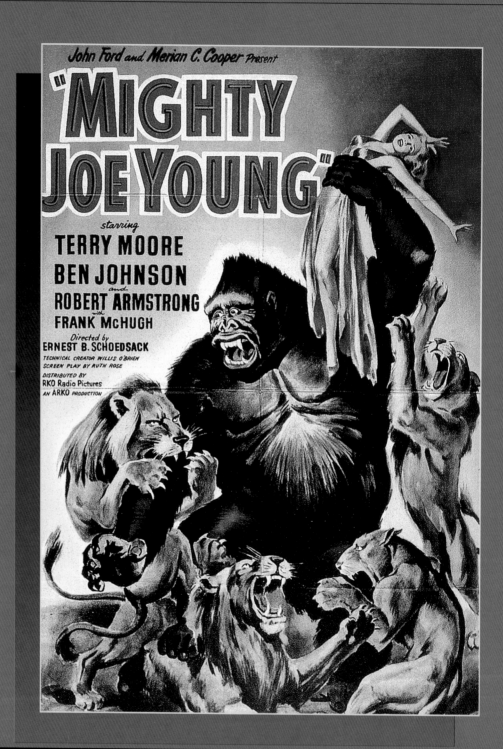

Mighty Joe Young *tells the story of a wild gorilla and his beautiful young owner when they are brought to New York to perform in nightclubs. The movie won an Academy award in 1949.*

Folklore

The gorilla has been an animal of mystery. It is often misunderstood and feared. People in both Africa and North America have used gorillas as a symbol of power. In Africa, gorillas have been hunted for food. Some hunters believed they could gain some of the gorilla's power by eating certain parts of its body. Some African tribes, such as the Lugbara of Uganda, have legends about cannibal heroes who were not quite human, but resembled men covered with long hair. These legends may have been based on encounters with gorillas.

King Kong *is probably the best-known movie about a gorilla. This movie made many North Americans believe that gorillas are dangerous and ferocious.*

Folklore History

Ancient Romans may have been the first non-Africans to see gorillas. Animals like gorillas are mentioned in Roman documents that are 2,500 years old. About 150 years ago, European explorers came in contact with "manlike monsters who could not converse with men." People wanted to know if there really were such creatures. Many early expeditions were sent out to shoot or capture these mysterious animals. Many gorillas were killed and collected in the name of science or adventure. It is only in the last few decades that people have begun to look beyond the gorilla's wild appearance, and have begun to understand its behavior.

Some people believe that the mysterious creature called the Abominable Snowman, or Yeti, is actually a large gorilla-like animal. In 1960 Sir Edmund Hillary, one of the first people to climb Mount Everest, unsuccessfully tried to prove that the Abominable Snowman existed. In North America, similar creatures have been called Bigfoot or Sasquatch.

Myths vs. Facts

Gorillas are ferocious and dangerous animals. They will attack and kill humans.

Gorillas are peaceful, gentle animals. They will, however, fight to protect themselves and their families. When gorillas have bitten or injured humans, they were usually acting in self-defense or protecting their young.

When gorillas pound their chests, it means they are angry and will attack you.

All gorillas, including infants, slap their chests. It can be an impressive display that often ends in a bluff charge rather than an actual attack. It can also be done in play, to show off, or to relieve stress.

The gorilla is a slow, lazy animal that spends most of its time sitting and eating.

Gorillas must spend a great deal of time eating. However, they are always alert to their environment and can move very quickly if danger threatens.

Folktales

Throughout history, gorillas have been misunderstood by the people who came into contact with them. In many old African legends, it is clear that gorillas are thought of as dangerous.

Dangerous Gorillas

Some African stories say gorillas are at war with humans. These stories suggest that gorillas will kidnap people and destroy villages if they have the chance. Some stories say that the spirits of dead people may turn into gorillas and live in the forest where they will harm people. Such stories may have grown from times when people attacked gorillas. Africans hunt gorillas for food and when gorillas raid their crops. Gorillas will fiercely defend their families, and can be very dangerous when threatened.

Powerful Gorillas

African stories also show that the gorilla is very strong. Some stories describe fierce battles between gorillas and leopards. The gorilla often defeats the leopard by swinging it in circles over its head until the leopard's tail comes off. Other stories tell how gorillas fight and defeat huge pythons.

Gorillas Related to People

In one legend of the Bulu tribe in the Cameroons, the gorilla is a brother of humans. The legend says that both the gorilla and humans were among God's five children. God gave all of his children fire, seeds, and tools. As the gorilla moved through the forest, he stopped to eat some fruit. By the time he had finished eating, his fire was out. God said that because of this, gorillas would have to live in the forest forever, and they would always have to flee from humans.

Gorilla Movies

In North America, gorillas became movie monsters. They were seen in movies with titles such as *Murders in the Rue Morgue, Bride of the Gorilla, Return of the Ape Man,* and *Gorilla at Large.*

King Kong is a famous movie about a giant gorilla. In this story, a 50-foot (15-m) gorilla named Kong lives on an island with prehistoric creatures. A team of hunters captures Kong and brings him to America so they can place him in an exhibit. Kong manages to escape, but he is killed by fighter planes as he climbs the Empire State Building in New York City.

More than 50 movies have been made with gorilla themes. Most portray gorillas as dangerous or stupid. A few have been more true to real gorillas. A movie called *Gorillas in the Mist* has been made about Dian Fossey's life with the mountain gorillas.

Gorilla Populations in Africa

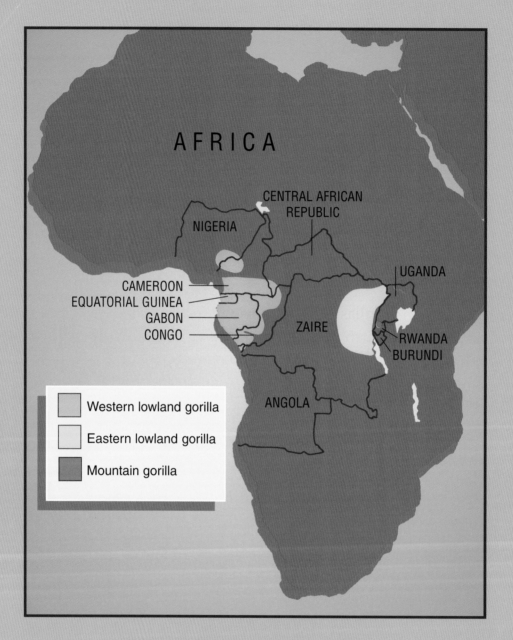

AFRICA

CENTRAL AFRICAN
REPUBLIC

NIGERIA

UGANDA

CAMEROON
EQUATORIAL GUINEA
GABON
CONGO

ZAIRE

RWANDA
BURUNDI

ANGOLA

Western lowland gorilla

Eastern lowland gorilla

Mountain gorilla

The three gorilla subspecies live in separate areas of Central Africa. As human populations grow, gorillas are forced to live in increasingly smaller areas.

Status

It is hard to know exactly how many gorillas there are in the wild because of their dense forest habitat.

Gorillas are threatened wherever they live in the wild. A serious threat to gorillas comes from the destruction of the forests in which they live. Another threat is hunting and poaching. Poaching occurs even in protected areas.

It is hard to know exactly how many gorillas there are in the wild because of their dense forest habitat. Mountain gorillas are the most endangered subspecies. There are only about 600 of them left in the world. These live in two populations that are separated by areas of human development.

Eastern lowland gorillas are also endangered. Only 3,000 to 5,000 of them live in small pockets of rain forest in Zaire. There are more Western lowland gorillas, but they are also threatened. About 40,000 of them live in the forests of West and Central Africa.

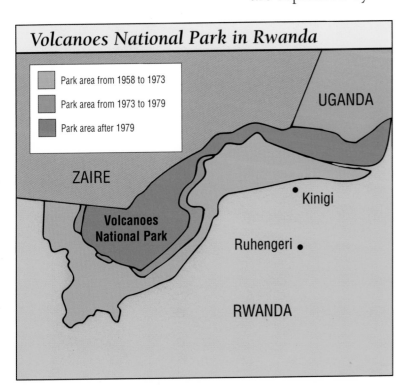

Volcanoes National Park in Rwanda

Park area from 1958 to 1973
Park area from 1973 to 1979
Park area after 1979

ZAIRE

UGANDA

Volcanoes
National Park

• Kinigi

Ruhengeri •

RWANDA

Although mountain gorillas are protected in Volcanoes National Park, park land has been shrinking steadily since 1958.

Poaching

Hunters who illegally kill animals in protected areas are called poachers. Poachers are a serious problem for gorillas. Poachers hunt gorillas with shotguns, rifles, spears, and arrows. Dogs are often used to track and hunt down gorillas.

Gorillas are sometimes injured by wire snares. These injuries may cause the gorilla to die or lose a finger, hand, or foot. The hands and heads of gorillas are sold by poachers. They are used as charms by local people, or are bought as souvenirs by tourists. Gorilla meat is thought to be a delicacy in some areas, and is sold in African markets.

In some areas, such as the Volcanoes National Park in Rwanda, there are special antipoaching patrols. Their job is to destroy poachers' snares and arrest any poachers they can find. This is often a very dangerous job. Some poachers will kill to protect their illegal trade.

Gorillas are sometimes caught by simple poachers' snares. Such snares are often used by poachers to catch animals, such as antelope. Many gorillas are accidentally caught and injured.

Gorillas in War

When civil war broke out in Rwanda in 1990, many people thought the mountain gorillas would not survive. The war lasted 4 years. It was a terrible time for the people living in Rwanda. Many thousands of people were killed, and many people lost their homes. Scientists studying gorillas at the Karisoke Research Center had to flee when the fighting got too close in 1994. Many of the Research Center's buildings and equipment were stolen or destroyed.

The gorillas, however, managed to survive, although not without some problems. Refugee camps with 800,000 people were crowding the edges of the park. There was a huge demand for firewood and food. Land mines had been left in the park, posing a threat to gorillas and people. When the fighting stopped, poaching started again. Several gorillas were killed. Many African trackers and rangers from both of the warring groups began the antipoaching patrols again.

The mountain gorillas have survived so far against great odds. If they are going to continue to survive, people from around the world will have to help the people of Rwanda solve their problems. The future of the Rwandan people and mountain gorillas are closely linked.

The war in Rwanda forced researchers to stop their work. When scientists returned to check on the research center in 1995, they were happy to see that young gorillas had been born. Many people had feared that the gorillas would not survive the war.

Viewpoints

Should gorillas be taught sign language?

Koko, a female gorilla at the Gorilla Foundation in Woodside, California, has been taught American Sign Language. She has learned over 800 signs that she uses to communicate with her human and gorilla companions. Koko seems to enjoy signing. She can ask for things and answer questions. Researchers working with Koko suggest that she can make up new words and even make jokes and insults. Some people say studies like these open a bridge between gorillas and humans. Others say these studies are not scientific and should not be done.

PRO

1 Gorillas naturally use gestures. Those that learn sign language may teach it to other gorillas. This may open new ways of studying how gorillas communicate.

2 Through sign language, we can learn about a gorilla's thoughts and feelings. We can see how gorillas view the world, and we can understand gorillas better.

3 Gorillas are interesting and intelligent animals. Language studies may make more people aware of this. More people may then want to help save wild gorillas.

CON

1 Gorillas have their own natural communication system. They do not need human sign language to communicate with one another.

2 Gorillas are not really communicating when they use signs. Much of what apes like Koko do is imitation or watching their trainers for cues.

3 It takes a great deal of time and money to teach gorillas sign language. This money and time could be used to help save wild gorillas.

Saving the Mountain Gorilla

You can help gorillas by supporting organizations that are trying to save them. One such organization is the Dian Fossey Gorilla Fund. Dian Fossey was a gorilla researcher who studied mountain gorillas in their natural habitat.

In 1977 one of Dian Fossey's favorite gorillas, Digit, was killed trying to defend his family from poachers. As a result, Fossey started the "Digit Fund" to protect the last wild mountain gorillas. It was renamed the "Dian Fossey Gorilla Fund" in 1992, in memory of the gorilla researcher.

The fund employs 30 Rwandans in antipoaching patrols, and as trackers and research assistants. These patrollers look for poachers and destroy thousands of snares each year. In 1985 there were fewer than 250 gorillas in the park. Many were being killed by poachers. The patrols seem to be helping since there are now about 400 gorillas in the park.

The Dian Fossey Gorilla Fund also supports research to help save gorillas. Many scientists and students study gorillas at the Karisoke Research Center. The Fossey Fund also helps to teach Rwandans about the mountain gorillas so they will want to save them.

Dian Fossey spent years observing mountain gorillas. During her research, she tried not to interfere with the gorillas, who eventually came to accept her presence.

What You Can Do

Gorillas are fascinating animals that need our help. You can learn more about gorillas by joining or writing to a conservation organization for more information.

Conservation Groups

INTERNATIONAL

World Wide Fund for Nature
Avenue du Mont Blanc
CH-1196 Gland
Switzerland

The Dian Fossey Gorilla Fund International
45 Inverness Dr. E., Suite B
Englewood, CO
80112

International Primate Protection League
P.O. Box 766
Summerville, SC
29484

UNITED STATES

African Wildlife Foundation
1717 Massachusetts Avenue N.W.
Washington, DC
20036

The Gorilla Foundation
P.O. Box 620-530
Woodside, CA
94062

World Wildlife Fund United States
1250 24th Street N.W.
Washington, DC
20037

International Wildlife Coalition
70 East Falmouth Highway
East Falmouth, MA
02536

CANADA

World Wildlife Fund Canada
90 Eglington Avenue E.
Suite 504
Toronto, ON
M4P 2Z7

Twenty Fascinating Facts

1 When gorillas shake their heads from side to side, it shows that they are getting ready to display. It is like they are saying, "Watch out!"

2 Nettles are one of the gorilla's favorite foods. This plant has tiny stinging hairs that cause painful red swellings on humans. Gorillas simply wipe off the hairs with their fingers and do not seem to be bothered by the stings.

3 Gorillas like to sunbathe. They will lie on either their front or back with their legs and arms outstretched in the sun for 2 or more hours at a time.

4 Gorillas and humans are alike in many ways. Gorillas can snore, hiccup, burp, cough, sneeze, scratch, and pick their noses.

5 Gorilla noses are so distinctive that observers use pictures of gorillas, called nose prints, to tell them apart. They look at how broad and high the nose is, the shape and spacing of the nostrils, and any scars and wrinkles.

6 Gorillas have rarely been observed drinking water in the wild. It is thought that they get all the moisture they need from plants.

7 Just as with humans, staring directly at a gorilla for a long time may cause it to feel threatened or uncomfortable.

8 Gorilla females have an average of 3 offspring in their lifetime that will survive.

9 Adult gorillas are very tolerant of infants playing on them and around them. The young ones can become great pests at times, biting, punching, pulling hair, and climbing up and sliding down the adult's body. When an adult has had enough play, it will sometimes lean on the infant until it stops.

10 Gorillas cannot swim, and they are reluctant to even enter shallow water. They have been seen using logs or stones to cross creeks that are only 1 or 2 feet (.3 or .6 m) deep.

11 Blackback male gorilla voices change, just like the voices of teenage human boys. Blackbacks will sometimes scream like female gorillas. At other times, they make a squeaky version of an adult male roar.

12 Gorillas are so large that few predators, except for humans, risk attacking an adult gorilla. However, there have been cases of leopards that have attacked and killed gorillas. One leopard killed four members of the same group at different times.

13 Twin gorillas have been born on occasion in zoos. There is also one record of twins being born in the wild, but they did not survive. Almost all gorilla births are single infants.

14 Gorillas need to eat large quantities of bulky plants in order to get enough nutrition for their big bodies. They spend 6 or 7 hours each day eating.

15 A gorilla can build a ground nest in 30 seconds or less. It may take up to 5 minutes to make a tree nest.

16 Male gorillas will sometimes adopt older, orphaned infants. They travel together and share a sleeping nest. Males may also groom the infants, but this is not something they are used to doing. Infants adopted by males can look quite scruffy.

17 Gorillas are so much like humans that doctors can help veterinarians solve gorilla health problems. In 1981 an infant gorilla at the Metro Toronto Zoo in Canada was found to have a brain abscess. She was successfully operated on by doctors at the Toronto Hospital for Sick Children. She had to wear a protective helmet for several months.

18 Some gorilla vocalizations sound like those of other animals. They have a call like a cat's purr. Other calls sound like a dog's bark and a horse's neigh.

19 Gorillas sometimes get caught in poachers' snares. Although some are able to recover, others die from their injuries or are permanently maimed. There are wild gorillas with missing or deformed fingers, hands, or feet because of snares.

20 In some African tribes, it is considered cowardly to have gorilla bites on your buttocks or legs. That is because when a gorilla runs toward a person it is usually a bluff charge. If the person stands his or her ground, the gorilla will stop or run past them. However, if the person turns and runs, the gorilla may chase them and bite the closest part of the running person.

Glossary

blackback: An adolescent male gorilla whose back has not yet turned silver

folivore: An animal that eats mainly the leaves and stems of plants

genetic evidence: The results of tests that examine genes to discover the origin or development of a species. Genes are the building blocks for making living things.

gestation period: The length of time that a female is pregnant

herbivore: An animal that eats only plants

home range: The entire area in which a gorilla group lives

knuckle-walking: A special way of moving. The gorilla's feet are flat on the ground, and its body weight is carried on its knuckles.

opposable: The ability to place either the first finger and thumb, or the big and second toes together to grasp things

poaching: Killing an animal illegally

primates: A large category of animals that includes prosimians, monkeys, apes, and humans

sagittal crest: A large, bony crest on the top of a gorilla's head to which its jaw muscles are attached

silverback: An adult male gorilla that has a saddle-shaped area of silver hair on its back

vocalizations: Sounds made to send messages to others or that express emotions

weaned: When a young gorilla does not drink milk from its mother anymore

Suggested Reading

Bourne, Geoffrey, and Maury Cohen. *The Gentle Giants*. New York: G.P. Putnam's Sons, 1975.

Fossey, Dian. *Gorillas in the Mist*. Boston: Houghton Mifflin Co., 1983.

Goodall, Alan. *The Wandering Gorillas*. London: Collins, 1979.

Kim, Melissa. *The Mountain Gorilla*. London: Random House, 1994.

McClung, Robert. *Gorilla*. New York: William Morrow and Co., 1984.

Nichols, Michael, and George Schaller. *Gorilla: Struggle for Survival in the Virungas*. New York: Aperture Foundation, 1989.

Redmond, Ian. *Gorilla*. Toronto: Stoddart Pub., 1995.

Schaller, George. *The Mountain Gorilla: Ecology and Behavior*. Chicago: University of Chicago Press, 1963.

Schaller, George. *The Year of the Gorilla*. Chicago: University of Chicago Press, 1964.

Index